Su has been happily married to Darren for over 30 years and has two grown up children, Emma and Lucas. They live in a small village in rural Hertfordshire, and being part of the village community is very important to Su. Having entertained her children by reading together as they grew up, she has charmed her family and friends with her comical rhymes for many years, and now has finally taken the next step to bring her humorous rhyming stories to a much wider audience.

To Emily, Jessica & Robin

There's always time
to rhyme!

Su Murray

Shirley Murley

Su Murley

AUSTIN MACAULEY PUBLISHERS™
LONDON · CAMBRIDGE · NEW YORK · SHARJAH

A CIP catalogue record for this title is available from the British Library.

ISBN 9781035805457 (Paperback)
ISBN 9781035805464 (ePub e-book)

www.austinmacauley.com

First Published 2023
Austin Macauley Publishers Ltd®
1 Canada Square
Canary Wharf
London
E14 5AA

To Darren, Emma, Lucas and all my lovely family and friends who have listened to my comical rhymes over the years. Thank you for giving me the confidence to publish.

Mr and Mrs Murley
live in Burnley.

They have a little girl
called Shirley.

Here is Shirley Murley
from Burnley.

Shirley does not like to be late.
She likes to be an early Shirley.

Here is always-early
Shirley Murley from
Burnley.

Shirley has curly hair. She is a curly Shirley. Here is curly Shirley who does not like to be late.

Welcome always-early, curly Shirley Murley from Burnley.

Shirley has a busy, busy life. She likes the hurly-burly. She is a hurly-burly Shirley.

With her curly hair and as she is never late, she is an always-early, hurly-burly, curly Shirley Murley from Burnley.

Shirley likes to dance. She becomes a swirly Shirley. Her hair sways, she is never late and she likes the hustle and bustle of her life.

She is an always-early, swirly, hurly-burly, curly, Shirley Murley from Burnley.

Shirley likes to spin. She becomes a twirly Shirley. She likes to dance, her hair sways, she is never late and she likes the hustle and bustle of her life.

She is an always-early, twirly, swirly, hurly-burly, curly Shirley Murley from Burnley.

Sometimes Shirley spins so fast she becomes whirly. Shirley is a whirly Shirley. She likes to spin and dance, her hair sways, she is never late and she likes the hustle and bustle of her life.

She is an always-early, whirly, twirly, swirly, hurly-burly, curly Shirley Murley from Burnley.

Shirley likes to wear her mummy's pretty pearl necklaces. She is a pearly Shirley. She spins and spins, she likes to dance, her hair sways, she is never late and she likes the hustle and bustle of her life.

She is an always-early, pearly, whirly, twirly, swirly, hurly-burly, curly Shirley Murley from Burnley.

What a very lovely little Shirley
Murley she is.

THE END